DINOSAUR
FOR A DAY

by Jim Murphy

Illustrated by
Mark Alan Weatherby

SCHOLASTIC INC.

New York   Toronto   London   Auckland   Sydney

The
author
wishes to
acknowledge and
thank Robert T. Bakker,
adjunct curator of paleontology
at the University of Colorado Museum,
for his insights into dinosaur mobility, and
John R. Horner, curator of paleontology at Montana
State University's Museum of the Rockies, for details
about Hypsilophodon nesting habits and
parental care. He also wishes to thank
Dr. Paul Sereno, assistant professor
of anatomy at the University
of Chicago, for checking
factual details
in the
text.

ISBN 0-590-92126-6

Text copyright © 1992 by Jim Murphy.
Illustrations copyright © 1992 by Mark Alan Weatherby.
All rights reserved. Published by Scholastic Inc.
BLUE RIBBON is a registered trademark of Scholastic Inc.

12 11 10 9 8 7 6 5 4 3 2 1   9   6 7 8 9/9 0 1/0

Printed in the U.S.A.   08

Designed by Marijka Kostiw

Mark Alan Weatherby's artwork
is done with a series of
acrylic washes
on paper.

DINOSAUR FOR A DAY

by **Jim Murphy**

Illustrated by

Mark Alan Weatherby

SCHOLASTIC INC.

New York   Toronto   London   Auckland   Sydney

The
author
wishes to
acknowledge and
thank Robert T. Bakker,
adjunct curator of paleontology
at the University of Colorado Museum,
for his insights into dinosaur mobility, and
John R. Horner, curator of paleontology at Montana
State University's Museum of the Rockies, for details
about Hypsilophodon nesting habits and
parental care. He also wishes to thank
Dr. Paul Sereno, assistant professor
of anatomy at the University
of Chicago, for checking
factual details
in the
text.

ISBN 0-590-92126-6

Text copyright © 1992 by Jim Murphy.
Illustrations copyright © 1992 by Mark Alan Weatherby.
All rights reserved. Published by Scholastic Inc.
BLUE RIBBON is a registered trademark of Scholastic Inc.

12 11 10 9 8 7 6 5 4 3 2 1   9   6 7 8 9/9 0 1/0

Printed in the U.S.A.   08

Designed by Marijka Kostiw

Mark Alan Weatherby's artwork
is done with a series of
acrylic washes
on paper.

You Can Be A Dinosaur

Did you know that over 340 kinds of dinosaurs existed during their long stay on Earth? Some of them were so small you could hold them in your hand. Others were as tall as a five-story building. Because scientists have been studying dinosaurs for over 200 years, we know what most of them looked like, what they ate, where they lived, and how they moved around.

All of this information gives us a good idea of what a typical dinosaur's day might have been like. If you have ever wondered what it would be like to be a dinosaur, here is your chance. You will see and experience this world through the eyes of a dinosaur named Hypsilophodon (which is pronounced HIP-sigh-LOAF-owe-don).

A Hypsilophodon weighed around 90 pounds and measured almost seven feet long from the tip of its nose to the end of its tail. Because it stood and walked leaning forward, its eyes were only about three and a half feet off the ground. When it had to, Hypsilophodon could stretch its neck up over bushes to see what was going on.

Hypsilophodon had small teeth, but it didn't use them to attack or eat other dinosaurs. It ate plants for food, and its teeth were for chewing tough leaves and branches.

Hypsilophodon's world was crowded with many other creatures. Tiny mammals and snakes hid under shrubs and bushes, while birds and pterosaurs flew between the trees. Swarms of insects filled the air. And, of course, there were other dinosaurs.

Most of these animals and insects did not bother Hypsilophodon. They just wanted to find food and be left alone. But there were a lot of ferocious meat-eating dinosaurs roaming the forests, and a Hypsilophodon was the kind of tasty meal they liked best.

How did a small and defenseless dinosaur like Hypsilophodon survive? For one thing, it lived with other Hypsilophodon. Each member of the group was alert for danger and would signal the others of its approach. It was also a very nervous animal. A strange noise would make it jumpy. Movement in the shadows would make it tense and ready to run.

That's all you really need to know for now. When you turn the page, your day as a Hypsilophodon begins.

It is early morning, and a misty rain is falling. The Hypsilophodon wakes, but it does not move. It stays close to the ground, listening. A hungry Troödon might be nearby waiting for it to leave its children unguarded.

The sounds are all familiar ones—insects buzzing, rain dripping off leaves, the squawks of other Hypsilophodon. Still, the Hypsilophodon raises its head slowly to peer over the bushes. Everything seems safe.

The Hypsilophodon's eight children are awake, too. They are four months old and very hungry. Another day has come, and it is time to find food.

The tastiest leaves on the island have already been eaten. The Hypsilophodon begins the search for tender shoots and sweet flowers. Its children follow.

The rain stops, and sunlight pokes through the trees. The Hypsilophodon tugs at a large leaf. Suddenly the bush shakes violently, and a grumpy Maiasaura appears. It is not happy to be disturbed and snorts a warning.

The Hypsilophodon scurries away, and its children try to stay close. At the water they all take a drink. The Hypsilophodon checks for danger on the other side. It sees none, so they wade across to the forest.

The woods are full of other Hypsilophodon families. There aren't enough plants to go around. The Hypsilophodon and its children follow a narrow path.

The ground is wet. The Hypsilophodon does not like the feel of the mud between its toes. It is startled by a loud *Snap!* nearby.

It listens and hears the noise again. *Snap! Snap!* The Hypsilophodon pushes through the leaves and finds itself staring at a giant Sauropelta.

The Sauropelta does not care about the Hypsilophodon. Instead, it opens its mouth and waits for insects to fly by. *Snap!* Then it swallows its meal. The Hypsilophodon turns to look for dry ground.

They go over a hill. The
ground gets hard and rocky.
No plants grow here.
Besides, the tall rocks make the
Hypsilophodon nervous. An enemy
might be hiding behind one.

To find a better feeding place, the
Hypsilophodon will have to cross a
wide stream. Fallen trees are the only
bridge to the other side. One at a
time, they jump onto the tree.

The tree is narrow, but the
Hypsilophodon's long tail helps it
keep its balance. Halfway across, a
shadow swoops down. The
Hypsilophodon ducks, and a
pterosaur's sharp beak barely
misses its head.

The pterosaur circles around and
lands on its nest. Its dark eyes glare.
The Hypsilophodon hurry across and
into the safety of the forest.

They come to a clearing filled with ferns and begin eating. The Hypsilophodon watches its children so they don't wander far.

In the middle of chewing a frond, it looks up. The forest is very quiet. Too quiet. Something is out there, watching them and waiting.

Its eyes search every shadow for movement. It listens for any noise. The children are nervous, too, and move closer for protection.

Then a terrible screech echoes through the forest.

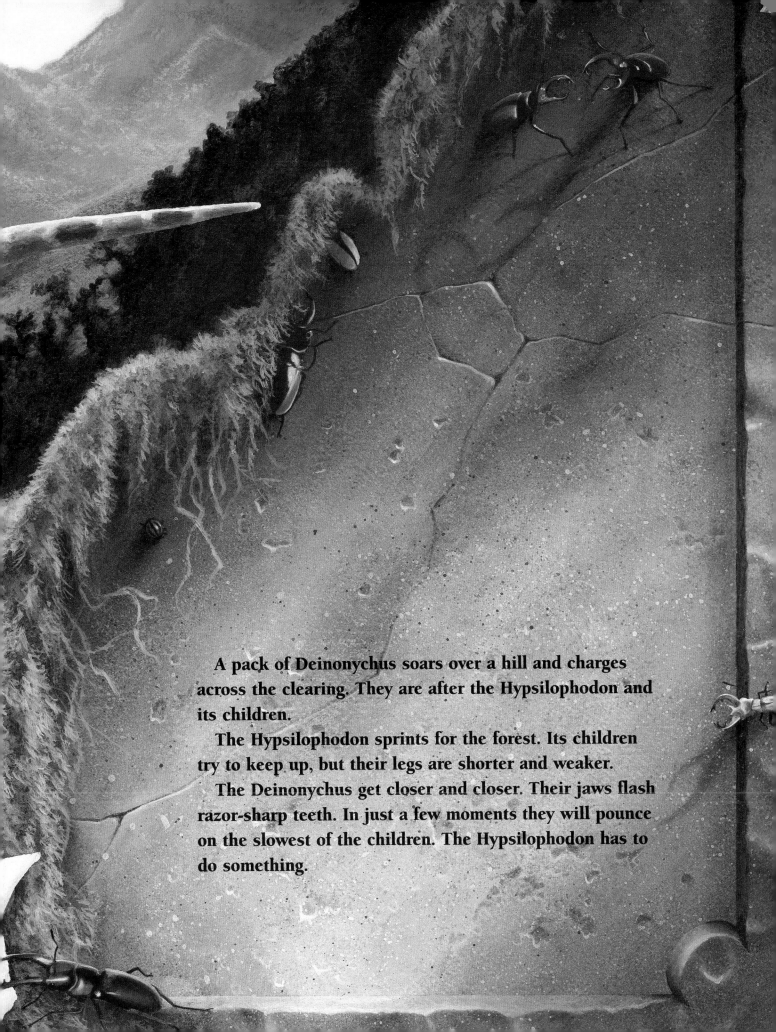

A pack of Deinonychus soars over a hill and charges across the clearing. They are after the Hypsilophodon and its children.

The Hypsilophodon sprints for the forest. Its children try to keep up, but their legs are shorter and weaker.

The Deinonychus get closer and closer. Their jaws flash razor-sharp teeth. In just a few moments they will pounce on the slowest of the children. The Hypsilophodon has to do something.

When it is a few steps from the forest, the Hypsilophodon digs its toes into the ground and turns. It runs away from the trees. The Deinonychus chase it, while the children escape into the thick forest.

The Hypsilophodon races through the ferns, jumping over the roots of a tree. The Deinonychus are right behind it.

The Hypsilophodon's legs are growing tired and heavy. It has to get away from its enemies very soon. It spots a path into the forest and goes down it. The Deinonychus spread out, dodging around trees and rocks and bushes. One is only a few feet behind the Hypsilophodon and getting closer.

Just then, a Deinonychus charges from the right side and leaps at the Hypsilophodon.

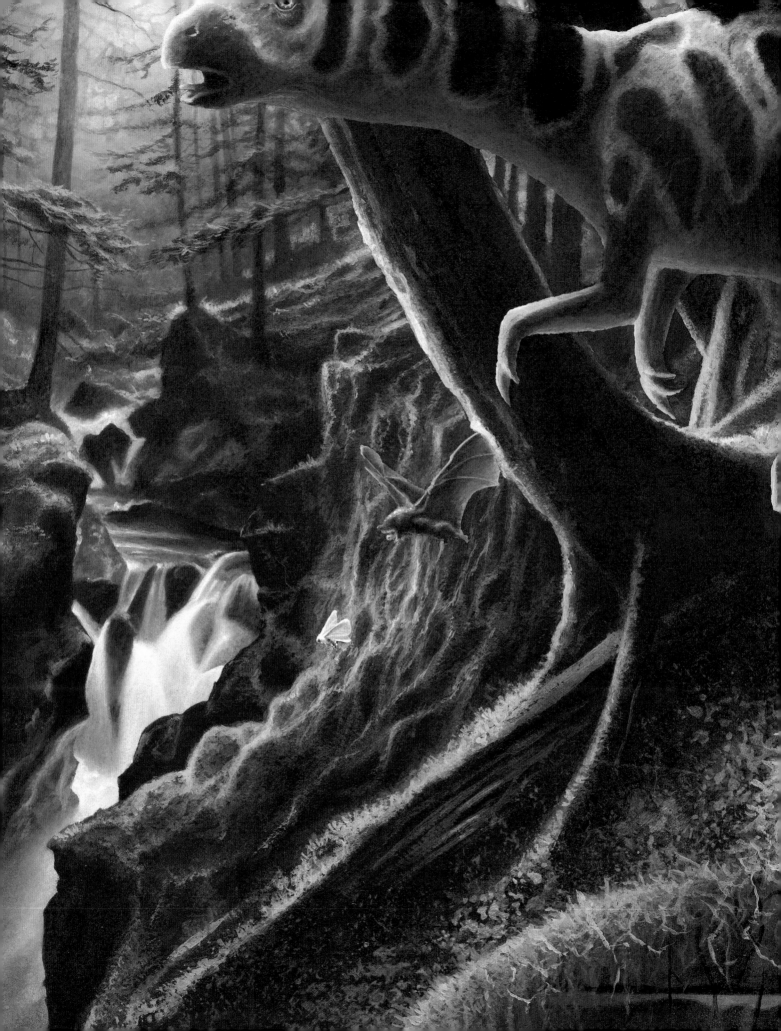

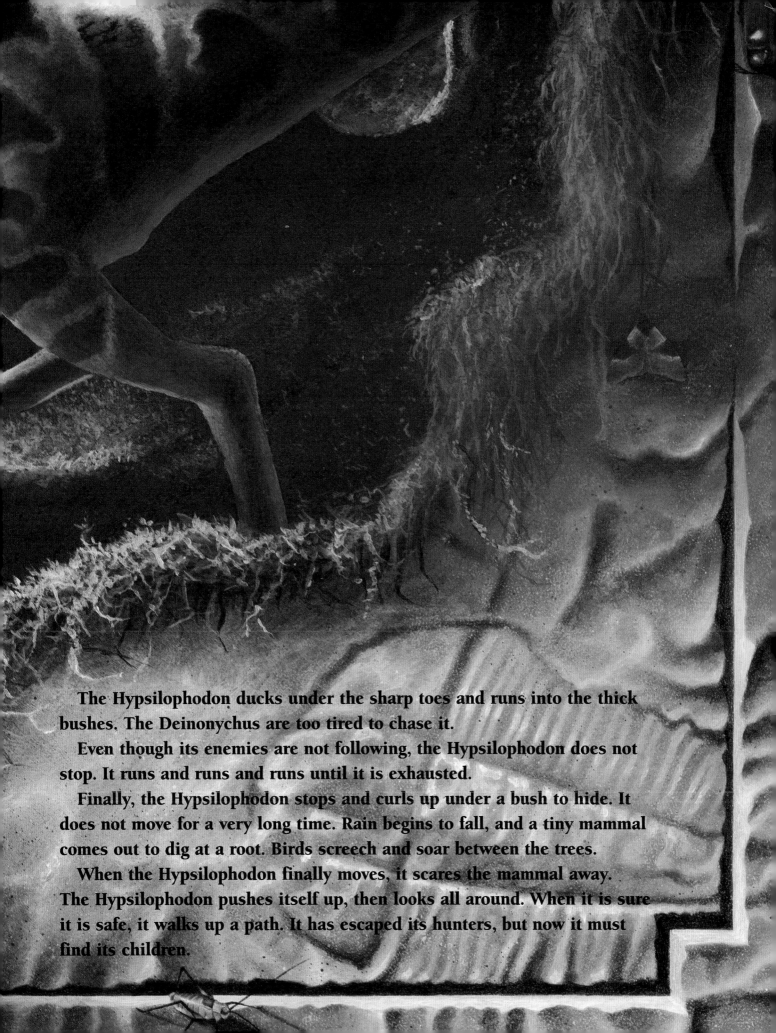

The Hypsilophodon ducks under the sharp toes and runs into the thick bushes. The Deinonychus are too tired to chase it.

Even though its enemies are not following, the Hypsilophodon does not stop. It runs and runs and runs until it is exhausted.

Finally, the Hypsilophodon stops and curls up under a bush to hide. It does not move for a very long time. Rain begins to fall, and a tiny mammal comes out to dig at a root. Birds screech and soar between the trees.

When the Hypsilophodon finally moves, it scares the mammal away. The Hypsilophodon pushes itself up, then looks all around. When it is sure it is safe, it walks up a path. It has escaped its hunters, but now it must find its children.

For hours the Hypsilophodon searches. Every once in a while, it stops to listen for them or squawks to see if they are near. There is never an answer.

Darkness comes to the forest. The Hypsilophodon has to move very slowly. At last, it comes to the clearing.

What if the Deinonychus are near? The Hypsilophodon stands still, listening. All it hears is the rain falling.

At last it calls out. Trees move back and forth and there is a rumble of thunder.

It calls again. This time, there is a faint answer.

The Hypsilophodon moves toward the sound, calling every few steps. Each time it hears an answer it moves toward it. Finally it finds all of its children huddled under the roots of a tree.

The Hypsilophodon does not like being near the clearing. It needs to find the island where it lives and the safety of its nest.

It prods its children along the path. Soon, it comes to the stream and the fallen trees. The trees are slippery in the rain, but they make it across. They travel through the tall rocks, and along the edge of the marsh to the water. It does not take long to wade across and find their way up to the nest.

A few Hypsilophodon look to see who has entered the nesting area. Most of the others are asleep. The Hypsilophodon and its family settle into the nest.

One at a time, the children drift off to sleep. Only the smallest is still awake and shivering.

The Hypsilophodon moves next to the little dinosaur to keep it warm. In time, its shivering stops and it, too, falls asleep.

The Hypsilophodon checks once more to make sure its children are safe. Then it curls up and closes its eyes.

Far away, some fierce creature screeches, and the Hypsilophodon's eyes pop open. It raises its head to look over the bushes. Nothing is moving in the darkness.

The Hypsilophodon settles down and closes its eyes again. The rain falls softly, dripping from leaf to leaf until it plops to the ground. Soon the Hypsilophodon is fast asleep. Another day has come to an end.

ONE SMART DINOSAUR

Many people might think the Hypsilophodon was a coward for running away from its enemies. It should have stayed and fought them, they might say. But what do you think would have happened if the Hypsilophodon had stood its ground? You're right. It—and all of its children—would have made an easy and delicious meal for the Deinonychus.

Instead, the Hypsilophodon used all of the weapons it had to detect and escape the sharp teeth and toes of its enemies. Even though it was eating, the Hypsilophodon was still alert enough to sense danger nearby. The instant it saw the Deinonychus, it sprinted away. And when it realized that its children would be caught, it was clever enough and fast enough to turn and lure the Deinonychus into chasing it.

In its race against Deinonychus the Hypsilophodon relied on its long, stiff tail to stay balanced as it leaped and turned while running. The Deinonychus were fast runners, too. But the Hypsilophodon's small size and light weight made it a step or two faster. In fact, a Hypsilophodon was probably one of the fastest dinosaurs of all time.

Obviously, a dinosaur's day was both hard and dangerous, and our Hypsilophodon had to be very skilled to survive. But it did survive! Some scientists estimate that Hypsilophodon and its many relatives may have flourished for almost 100 million years. That makes it one of the smartest and most successful dinosaurs ever to have lived!

SAY THAT AGAIN

Dinosaur names are usually taken from Latin or ancient Greek and can sometimes be very hard to say. Below you'll find a pronunciation guide to the dinosaurs mentioned in this story, as well as some additional facts about them. Say the names slowly several times. Then say them a little faster. With practice, even the name Deinonychus will become easy to say.

Deinonychus (DIE-no-NICK-us) was a speedy meat-eater that grew to a length of 13 feet and weighed around 200 pounds. Its name means "terrible claw" and refers to its sharp, sickle-shaped claws and toes. These fierce hunters roamed the countryside in packs, running down slower-moving dinosaurs.

Hypsilophodon (HIP-sigh-LOAF-owe-don) had short arms with five-fingered hands, and long sprinter's legs. Its name means "high ridge tooth" and refers to its long, self-sharpening teeth, which allowed it to chew a great variety of plants. Hypsilophodon built nests together and cared for their young for several months after they were born.

Maiasaura (MY-ah-SAW-rah) was a 30-foot-long plant-eater. It had no real defense against attack, though when annoyed it could stand very tall on its hind legs and try to scare away enemies. If that didn't work, it could run into the cover of the trees. Maiasaura means "good mother lizard," and there is evidence that it brought food back to its nest of babies.

Pterosaur (TE-row-soar) means "flying reptile." Some were as small as sparrows, while others had wingspans of almost 40 feet. Modern research suggests that, despite their ungainly appearance, these creatures were powerful and agile fliers and probably lived near water.

Sauropelta (SAW-row-PELL-tah) was huge, 25 feet long and weighing as much as three and a half tons. Its name means "lizard shield" and refers to bands of large and small shields that ran across its back. For additional protection, it also had rows of spikes along its back and tail. Sauropelta ate soft, low-growing plants, but probably liked to snack on insects.

Troödon (TRUE-eh-don) was about the same size as Hypsilophodon and looked a lot like it but had very sharp teeth for cutting flesh. In fact, its name means "wounding tooth." It might have hid near nesting areas and waited for dinosaur parents to leave their children unguarded. Then it would sprint to the nest and snatch a child away.

SOME BOOKS ABOUT DINOSAURS

There have been hundreds of books written about dinosaurs. Here is a brief list of some very good sources of information about these fantastic creatures. Most of these books contain lots of illustrations, as well as maps, diagrams, and the names of museums that contain dinosaur fossils.

Bakker, Robert T. *The Dinosaur Heresies: New Theories Unlocking the Mystery of the Dinosaurs and Their Extinction.* New York: William Morrow and Company, 1986.

Booth, Jerry. *The Big Beast Book: Dinosaurs and How They Got that Way.* Boston: Little, Brown and Company, 1988.

Charig, Alan. *A New Look At The Dinosaurs.* London: Heinemann, 1979.

Czerkas, Sylvia, ed. *Dinosaurs Past and Present.* Los Angeles: Los Angeles County Museum Press, 1986.

Glut, Donald F. *The New Dinosaur Dictionary.* Secaucus, New Jersey: Citadel Press, 1982.

Horner, John R. "Evidence of Colonial Nesting and 'Site Fidelity' Among Ornithischian Dinosaurs." *Nature*, Vol. 297, 1982.

Horner, John R. and James Gorman. *Digging Dinosaurs.* New York: Harper and Row, 1988.

Lambert, David. *A Field Guide to Dinosaurs.* New York: Avon Books, 1983.

Swinton, W.E. *The Dinosaurs.* New York: Wiley, 1970.

Swinton, W.E. *The Wonderful World of Prehistoric Animals.* Garden City, New York: Garden City Books, 1971.

Wilford, John Noble. *The Riddle of the Dinosaurs.* New York: Alfred A. Knopf, 1985.